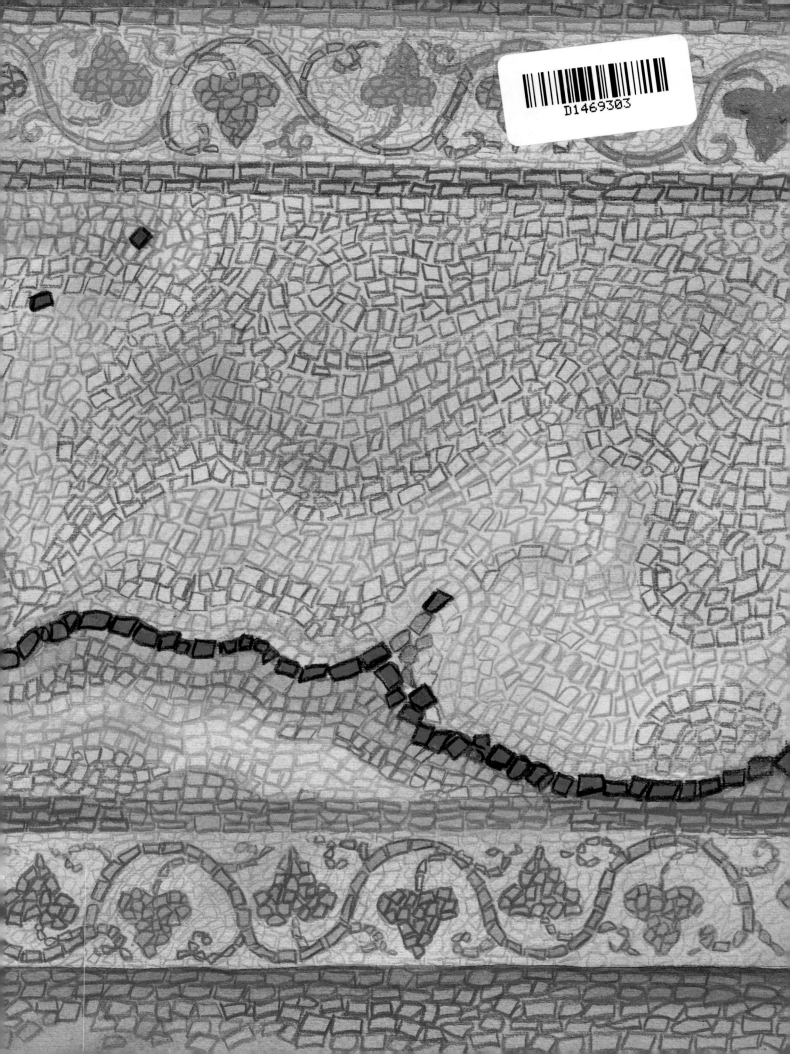

Catalogue
A catalogue of our editions is available on request from,
MSM B. P. 20 65500 Vic-en-Bigorre (France)
Tel.: (33) 62 96 72 02, Fax.: (33) 62 96 28 99

Dépôt légal: March 1996
ISBN: 2-909998-49-2
Printed in Belgium by Casterman SA, Tournai

Marcus

A child in Roman Provence

Drawings: Gemma Sales
Text: Jean Hennegé

Translated by Ann MacDonald-Plénacoste

"Can falcons feel sea-sick?"
wondered Marcus as he looked at Sagitta's dull feathers.
Marcus and his father, Lucius, had left Ostie, the port of
Rome, twenty days before. But although the young boy loved
sailing from port to port, his tame bird wasn't very happy
to find himself shut in a basket in the hold.
"Look, Sagitta – land! It's Gaul. And the port you can see is *Massilia*
where our sea voyage ends. You'll soon be free!"

Lucius, was a well-known craftsman. He designed mosaics and assembled
them piece by piece like big jig-saw puzzles made of glass and stone. A rich
merchant had asked him to come and decorate his home at *Vasio* in the
Narbonne region of Gaul, and Marcus, who longed to visit the provinces,
had managed to convince his father to take him along.
"I'd rather have crossed the ocean to visit Africa" said Marcus to himself.
"But Gaul isn't a bad start!"

"No, no! There are no lions in Gaul", laughed Lucius. Marcus was both reassured and a little disappointed. The road from *Massilia* to *Aquæ Sextiæ*, the first stage of their journey, was just as good as the roads in the suburbs of Rome. But it's true that this part of Gaul had been under Roman influence for a long time… Marcus had fun listening to the drivers joking amongst themselves: they were speaking Latin, but with such a strange accent!

"There's nothing like a nice bath after a tiring journey," Lucius told his son. The thermal baths at *Aquæ Sextiæ* were magnificently decorated; it was like being under the sea! Like in Rome, the water was supplied from heated cisterns by a network of lead pipes. People jostled around Lucius to hear the latest news from the capital. Even Marcus felt quite important!

At each halt in their journey, Marcus let Sagitta fly free. The countryside was so beautiful here that Marcus wished he could fly too. A white mountain, the Mount *Venturi*, towered above the plain where crops were gradually replacing the forest. Lucius told Marcus that the Roman army had gained a great victory over the Germanic tribes at the foot of this mass of rocks. Marcus found it difficult to imagine that this region had been a battle field a few centuries before. The countryside was so peaceful, and the bread and cheese were delicious! Marcus began to feel quite at home… even though the young Gaul, who was minding his pigs in the woods, did look at him rather warily.

Further north, the travellers stopped to admire the natural fountain at *vallis clausa*. Marcus knew that such places existed – magic places where gods and nymphs met in secret… Were they there at that very moment, hidden in the depths of the emerald green waters? Only a falcon with its piercing eye could say if this were so! But Sagitta did not betray the secrets of the gods…

The next day, another kind of magic awaited Marcus and his father. Glass-makers were turning sand into glass paste, which they then blew to shape goblets, bottles and richly coloured jewellery. Lucius was speechless with admiration when he noticed a shade of blue that he had never seen before. "Not even in Rome?", asked Marcus, astonished and a little offended for the craftsmen of his home town. Lucius left with his bag full of glass strips to be cut into cubes and used in his mosaics.

"Legionaries!
– I've already told you that legions are as rare as lions here! Gaul has been at peace for such a long time now…"
Astonished, the little boy's father stopped short in the middle of his explanation; these were indeed legionaries manoeuvring on the road ahead!

One of the guards explained the mystery: the Legion was preparing for Emperor Hadrian's visit to Gaul, which was to take place the following month. When the centurian gave the order, the legionaries went into the "turtle" formation. In no time at all, they were ready to deliver an attack, protected on all sides by the "shell" formed by their heavy wooden shields.

Vasio was a large town with wide paved streets. Lucius had no trouble finding the *domus* of Caius Julius Flavius, his future client. Only a few windows looked out onto the street, but some of them were glazed! The peristyle, in the centre of the house was the nicest place to talk in the early evening. The air was pleasantly cool by the pool and fountain and peacocks, strutting about freely, were showing off their magnificent plumage.

In the *triclinium*, the dining-room, the floor was being decorated with beautiful colours arranged in complicated patterns. Marcus cut cubes of marble, stone and glass which Lucius skilfully set in place on a bed of fine mortar. In the centre of the mosaic, the owner's favourite peacock, Leo, was depicted with his magnificent tail spread out.

"Now we don't have to wait ages for the real Leo to show off his tail", thought Marcus, who was a little annoyed by Leo's laziness.

The work had lasted for a whole month, and the mosaic was now finished. That evening there was a celebration in the *domus*. Caius Julius Flavius gave the guests wines to taste from his own vineyard. Strongly spiced and deliciously flavoured with honey, they were every bit as good as wines from Italy or Greece… but Lucius thought that Caius Julius Flavius was perhaps rather mean… In Rome, banquets were much more sumptious. The young slave who brought the dishes to the table reminded Marcus of Aemilia, his sister. The girl had rather a funny Gallic accent, but she looked kind and gentle… Marcus began to feel a little sad; she could never be his friend.
Why couldn't she have been born free like him?

More work awaited Lucius
at *Nemausus*. In the end, Caius Julius
Flavius had turned out to be very
generous. "Why don't we stop at
Arausio? We could go to the theatre…"
In the stone theatre at *Arausio*, it was a pleasure
to see the masked characters of the Roman plays.

Of course, Sagitta was first to see the Arc de Triomphe (the Triumphal Arch) and the mausoleum of Glanum. Intrigued, he circled it several times. But Marcus was fascinated by the sculptures of Gallic prisoners and the war scenes… to think that Gauls and Romans had fought so fiercely at that time! Now Roman peace reigned and the roads were safe "Fortunately, there will never be another war in Gaul!", sighed Marcus with relief.

Marcus had nevery seen such a wide and turbulent river as the *Rhodanus*. But he knew that no river, however terrible, could stop a Roman road. From the mysterious lands of Asia, from the rich colonies of Africa, or even from the Germanic lands lost in the northern mists, every road leading to Rome always managed to surmount any obstacle. Crossing the pontoon bridge, Marcus could see the busy port of *Arelate*. Ships loaded with goods from different countries sailed up the river here or reached the *Mare Nostrum* by canal.

"What can Sagitta be thinking while he's flying high over the city?",
wondered Marcus. "The humans crowded in these narrow streets must seem
so small to him! And what does he think of our passion for the theatre?
Or of the animal sounds coming from under the white linen canopy of the
amphitheatre when we watch wild beast shows? Elephants, lions, ostriches
or hippotamus must seem less strange to him than we do!"

"Come on the Red One!", shouted Marcus in the middle of the excited crowd. *Arelate* was one of the rare towns to have an amphitheatre. Four hundred metres long, it could hold over twenty thousand people. Lucius was as excited as Marcus about seeing a quadriga race; quadrigas were light two-wheeled chariots pulled by four horses. Four teams were fighting for victory, but Marcus hadn't chosen the right colour…

Marcus had already seen the driver of the red team of horses in Rome. He was one of the most famous drivers at the time and his name was Lucius too. From Brittany to Egypt, he had the reputation of being a risk-taker. But that day the champion didn't seem to be at his best. He came in third, in spite of the little boy's shouts of encouragement!

That morning, Marcus had sulked because his father had wanted to continue on foot instead of taking the carriage. But later on, he was happy to be able to swim in the cool waters of the river at the foot of the huge aquaduct carrying the water supply to *Nemausus*. Like most Gallo-roman towns, *Namausus* had running water, several fountains, public baths and even a drainage network to evacuate dirty water.

Sagitta let himself be carried by the warm air rising from the *forum*, the central square in *Nemausus*. He watched the comings and goings of the citizens as they met to discuss business or City life. He was also keeping an eye on his little master… Marcus was sitting in the shade of the Maison Carré, the temple where the cult of the emperor was celebrated.

A few streets away, a huge clamour arose together with the sound of trumpets and horns. Sagitta, inquisitive, raised one wing and slid through the air to the amphitheatre…

The gladiators were tearing each other apart in the dust of the arena. They fought using daggers, swords or tridents... Contrary to what Marcus believed, Sagitta had no opinion about men's behaviour. And when there was too much noise, he just flew a little higher...

Vines stretched as far as the eye could see all along the *via Domitia* leading to the large port of *Narbo Martius*.
"What a lot of wine these Gauls must drink", exclaimed Marcus.
Lucius laughed but didn't reply until later when they arrived in a large village where potters were making flat-bottomed jars by the thousand.
"Wine from the Narbonne region of Gaul is sent all over the Empire, from Germany to Egypt… in fact I think I'll have a good jar of *picatum* delivered to the house!".

Marcus could hardly wait to see his mother, his sister Aemilia and all his Roman friends again.
And while Sagitta, shut in his basket, was beginning to feel sea-sick once more, *Narbo Martius* and the shores of Gaul slowly disappeared into the mist...
As he looked at his father, Marcus said to himself "one day, I'll be a good mosaic craftsman too... And I'll come back!"

Monuments and works of art from Roman
Gaul still remain. Archaeologists are continually discovering
additional vestiges which provide a better idea of life at
that time… and often they patiently restore mosaics that are two
thousand years old… Perhaps some of these mosaics are the work
of a young craftsman whose tame white falcon was never far away…